Sophie
and the
Perfect
Poem

SEAN COVEY

Illustrated by Stacy Curtis

Ready-to-Read

Simon Spotlight
New York London Toronto Sydney New Delhi

To my daughter Beth, steady, accepting,
and a friend to everyone.
—Sean Covey

For my brother, Jeff
—Stacy Curtis

SIMON SPOTLIGHT
An imprint of Simon & Schuster Children's Publishing Division
1230 Avenue of the Americas, New York, New York 10020
This Simon Spotlight edition May 2020
Copyright © 2013 by Franklin Covey Co.
For information about special discounts for bulk purchases, please contact Simon & Schuster Special
Sales at 1-866-506-1949 or business@simonandschuster.com.
Manufactured in the United States of America 0420 LAK
2 4 6 8 10 9 7 5 3 1
Library of Congress Cataloging-in-Publication Data
Names: Covey, Sean, author. | Curtis, Stacy, illustrator.
Title: Sophie and the perfect poem / by Sean Covey ; illustrated by Stacy Curtis.
Description: New York : Simon Spotlight, 2020. | Series: The 7 habits of happy kids ; 6 | Audience:
Ages 5–7 | Summary: Ms. Hoot assigns Sophie and Biff as partners to write a poem, then encourages
Sophie to open her eyes to the possibility that Biff is not as mean and scary as he seems and has some
good ideas, too.
Identifiers: LCCN 2019041527 | ISBN 9781534444591 (paperback) | ISBN 9781534444607 (hardcover) |
ISBN 9781534444614 (eBook)
Subjects: CYAC: Cooperativeness—Fiction. | Schools—Fiction. | Squirrels—Fiction. | Animals—Fiction.
Classification: LCC PZ7.C8343 Sop 2020 | DDC [E]—dc23
LC record available at https://lccn.loc.gov/2019041527

At school one day,
Ms. Hoot said,
"Class, I am going to pair you up
with a partner.
You will write a poem together.
You will share the poem
with the class in one week."
Sophie hoped Lily
would be her partner.

Lily's partner was Pokey.
Allie and Sammy were matched up.
Goob and Jumper were made
partners.
"And Sophie and Biff will
work together," said Ms. Hoot.

Sophie couldn't believe it.
She didn't want to be partners
with Biff.
Biff was mean and scary.

Tagalong Allie felt sorry
that Sophie's partner was Biff.
"Yeah, that's a real bummer,"
said Jumper.

"I'm probably going to have
to write it all by myself,"
said Sophie.
"It has to be perfect."

The next day, Ms. Hoot
gave everyone time
to meet with their partners.
Sophie and Biff got together
in the corner by the fish tank.
"I think we should write a poem
about the sun, moon, and stars,"
said Sophie.

Biff did not like Sophie's idea one
bit. "I think we should write a poem
about trees, wind, and water!"
Biff yelled.
Sophie sighed.
This was going to be
even harder than she thought.

Sophie decided to talk
with Ms. Hoot.
"Can I please get a different partner?
Biff isn't very nice, and he doesn't
have any fresh ideas."

"Oh, my dear Sophie. If you get to know him, you'll find that Biff is really nice, and he has lots of good ideas, just like you. I'm sure you two can come up with a poem that will make you both proud. Just open your eyes," said Ms. Hoot.

Sophie agreed that she would try.

So Biff and Sophie started
working on their poem.
"What do you like about trees?"
asked Sophie.
"You can use them to make a beaver
dam. My dad made one that took
him six months, and I got to help."
"That's cool," said Sophie.

"I also like the sun, moon, stars, and all that stuff too," said Biff.
"You do?" asked Sophie.
They decided to put their ideas together. They got to work.

Over the next few days,
Sophie and Biff hardly
took a break.
They met by the creek.
Biff looked worried.

"I bet you have lots
of good ideas, Biff,"
said Sophie.
She asked him to share
some ideas with her.
She did the same with him.

Together they wrote
a few more poems.
The new poems were created
from the ideas they had shared
with each other.

Then they combined all their ideas
into one really great poem.

Each day, they practiced.
Biff read aloud
part of their poem.
Sophie sat quietly
and listened to him.
He did a great job.

The next day
it was Sophie's turn.
She read another part
of their poem.
Biff listened.
He really liked it!

The big day arrived.
It was time for everyone
to share their poems.
Goob and Jumper got up
in front of the class and
read their poem first.
It was called "Bugs and Basketballs."

"Here goes," said Goob.

Basketballs and little bugs
Everywhere you look.
Little bugs and basketballs
See them in a book.
If I had an ant
I would hide him in a plant.
If I had a ball
I would bounce it off a wall.
That would be real fun
Too bad this poem is done.

"Well, that was . . . ummm . . . interesting," said Ms. Hoot.

Next up were Sophie and Biff.
Biff nervously read their poem.
Sophie stood proudly by.
Their poem was called
"Open Your Eyes."

I opened my eyes and what did I see?
The sun, the moon, the stars, the trees.
I opened my ears and what did I hear?
A gentle breeze on water clear.
I opened my heart and what did I find?
An awesome new friend and a wonderful time.

Biff and Sophie gave
each other a high five.
The whole class cheered
for Biff and Sophie.

"Well, ruffle my feathers!"
said Ms. Hoot.
She proclaimed it a perfect poem!

"Wow, Sophie. Your poem
was really, really good.
I guess Biff wasn't so bad, huh?"
said Tagalong Allie.

"Hey, everyone,
let's play some soccer,"
Jumper called.
Sophie said, "Great!
Biff, are you coming?"

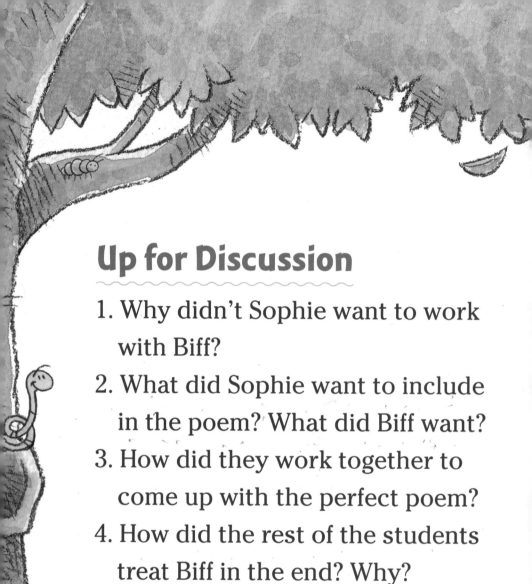

Up for Discussion

1. Why didn't Sophie want to work with Biff?

2. What did Sophie want to include in the poem? What did Biff want?

3. How did they work together to come up with the perfect poem?

4. How did the rest of the students treat Biff in the end? Why?

5. What does teamwork mean? Why is it important to include others?

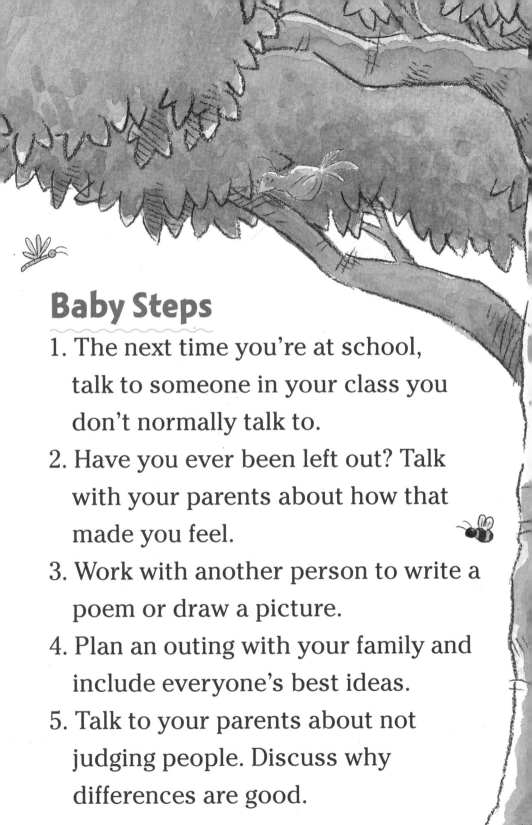

Baby Steps

1. The next time you're at school, talk to someone in your class you don't normally talk to.

2. Have you ever been left out? Talk with your parents about how that made you feel.

3. Work with another person to write a poem or draw a picture.

4. Plan an outing with your family and include everyone's best ideas.

5. Talk to your parents about not judging people. Discuss why differences are good.

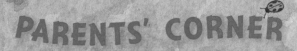

HABIT 6 —Synergize: *Together Is Better*

Synergy is when two or more people work together to create something better than either could alone, just like Sophie and Biff did when they wrote their poem. Unlike compromise, where 1 + 1 equals 1 ½, with synergy, 1 +1 can equal 3 or more. It's not your way or my way but a better way, a higher way. Builders know all about this. They know that one two-by-four beam can support 607 pounds, but two two-by-fours nailed together can support not just 1,214 pounds (which is what you'd expect), but a whopping 4,878 pounds! So it is with us. We can do so much more together than we can alone.

The fact is, we are all different in so many ways, and that's a wonderful thing. If we can learn to value our differences and see them as an advantage, instead of being afraid of them and seeing them as obstacles, we will get so much more accomplished—at home and work, in our marriages and friendships, or wherever life may lead.

In this story, point out how Sophie and the gang judged Biff without really knowing him. They thought he was mean and scary. In reality, he was just different. But once Sophie opened her eyes and really got to know Biff and valued his strengths, and Biff did the same with Sophie, good things happened.

So the next time someone disagrees with you, say, "That's good. I'm glad you see it differently."